my name is not Isabella

story by Jennifer Fosberry • pictures by Mike Litwin

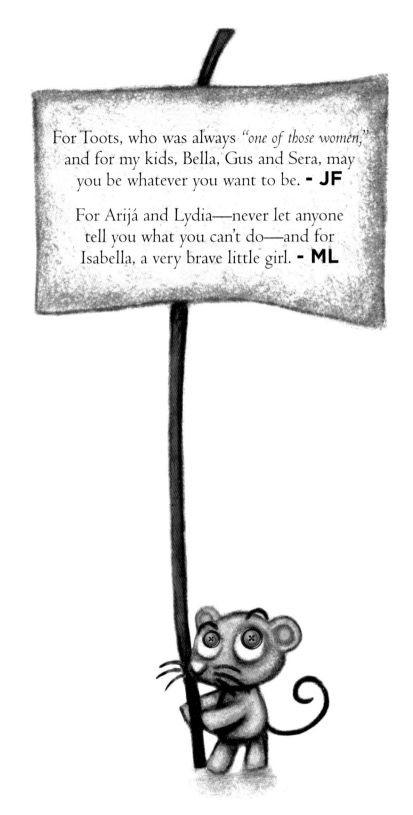

For Toots, who was always *"one of those women,"* and for my kids, Bella, Gus and Sera, may you be whatever you want to be. **- JF**

For Arijá and Lydia—never let anyone tell you what you can't do—and for Isabella, a very brave little girl. **- ML**

Text Copyright© 2008 Jennifer Fosberry
Illustration Copyright © 2008 Mike Litwin

Published by
Monkey Barrel Press
www.monkeybarrelpress.com

Printed in China

Publisher's Cataloging-in-Publication data

Fosberry, Jennifer.
    My name is not Isabella / story by Jennifer Fosberry; pictures by Mike Litwin.
    p. cm.
    Includes bibliographical references.
    ISBN 978-0-9802000-7-2
    Summary: From breakfast to bedtime, a young girl imagines being
        different women who made history, and ends the day
        empowered to be herself.
[1. Girls--Fiction. 2. Women--Fiction. 3. Biographical fiction.] I. Litwin, Mike. II. Title.

PZ .F7847 My 2008
[E]--dc22   2007942026

"Good morning, *Isabella*," the mother said.

"It's time to get up and out of bed."

"My name is not Isabella!" said the little girl.

"Then who has been sleeping in my daughter's bed?" asked the mother.

"I am SALLY,

he greatest, toughest astronaut who ever was!"

"Well Sally, BLAST out of bed, put on your spacesuit and come downstairs for breakfast."

"Good morning, Sally," the mother said. "It's time for breakfast, pull up a chair."

"My name is not Sally!" said the little girl.

"Then who will eat this fine breakfast I cooked?" asked the mother.

"Okay Annie," the mother said.
"It's time for school."

"My name is not Annie!"
said the little girl.

"Then who will go outside
and wait for the bus?"
asked the mother.

"Welcome home, Rosa," the mother said. "Did you have a nice day at school?"

"My name is not Rosa!" said the little girl.

"Then who will eat these
cookies I made while they
do their homework?"
asked the mother.

"I am **MARIE**, the greatest, smartest scientist who ever was!"

"Well Marie, sit down and **DISCOVER** the answers to your homework, and I will get the cookies."

"Time for dinner, Marie," the mother said. "Come help me set the table."

"My name is not Marie!" said the little girl.

"Then who will help me set out the dishes for our fine meal?" asked the mother.

"I am ELIZABETH, the greatest, kindest doctor who ever was!"

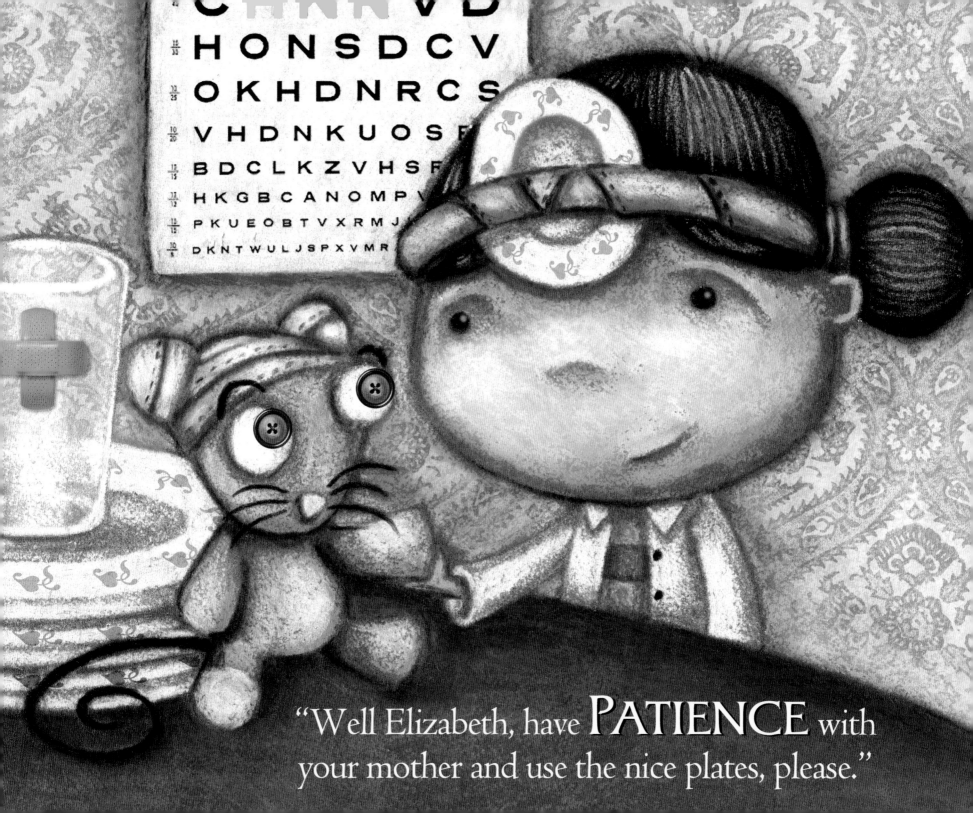

"Well Elizabeth, have PATIENCE with your mother and use the nice plates, please."

"It's almost bedtime, Elizabeth," the mother said. "Come upstairs and take your bath."

"My name is not Elizabeth!" said the little girl.

"Then who will relax in this nice hot bath I have drawn?" asked the mother.

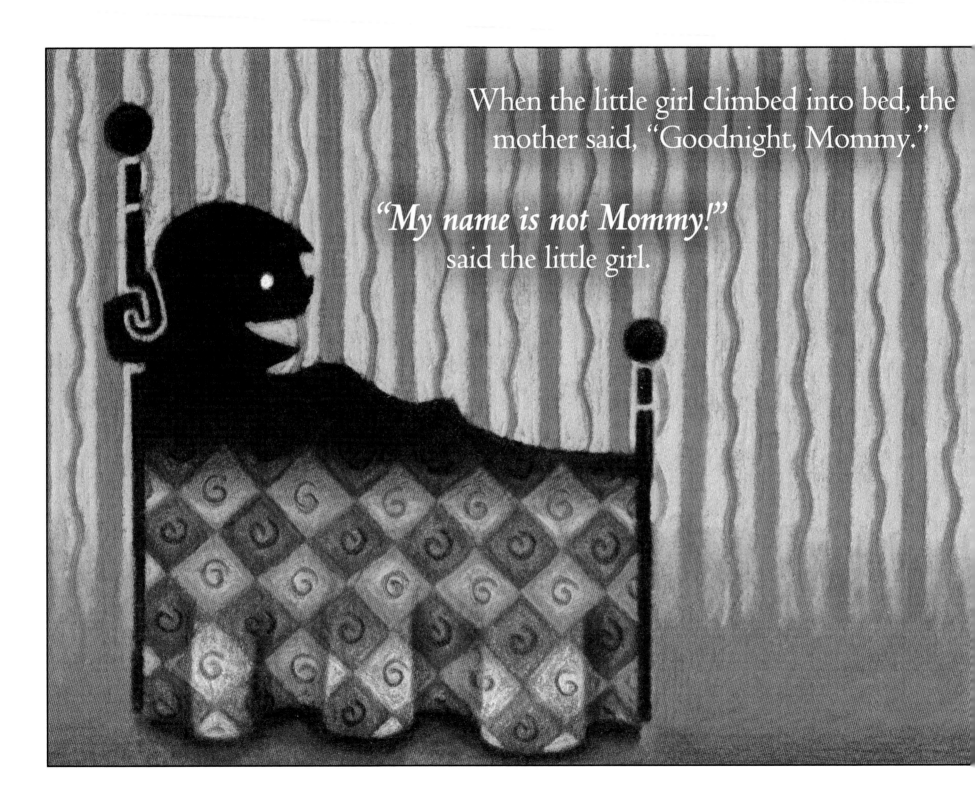

When the little girl climbed into bed, the mother said, "Goodnight, Mommy."

"My name is not Mommy!" said the little girl.

"Then who will be sleeping in my daughter's bed tonight?" asked the mother.

"It's me, *Isabella,* the sweetest, kindest, smartest, bravest, fastest, toughest, greatest girl that ever was," said the little girl as she fell asleep and dreamed about who she would be...

...tomorrow.

women who changed the world

SALLY RIDE (1951 -):

Sally Ride was the first woman from the United States to travel to space. She studied physics at Stanford University. In 1978, Sally was one of six women to join NASA to train for space missions. On June 18, 1983, she flew on the space shuttle Challenger. Her job was to test a robot arm. Since then Sally has been a teacher at many California Universities. She has started many programs to help kids become more interested in math, science and technology.

An **ASTRONAUT** is a person who does their work in space. There are different jobs on the spacecraft. Some people are pilots. Some people fix the spacecraft. Some people do science research.

ANNIE OAKLEY (1860-1926):

Annie Oakley was one of the first women superstars. When she was young, her family was poor. For many years, she had to live away from home at the poor farm. She also lived with another family and worked as a servant. When she came home her family was about to lose the farm. Annie hunted for small game and sold to the local town. When she was 15, she paid all the money for her Mother's house. Many people knew she was a very good shooter. When Frank Butler, a famous marksman, visited her town, he challenged anyone to a shooting contest. Annie won the prize and later married Frank Butler. One time Annie filled in with Frank for his shooting show. Soon they knew Annie was much better at the show, so she became the star. Annie traveled with the "Buffalo Bill's Wild West" show. She traveled and performed in America and Europe. Annie told people that she fought to be able to compete and perform as a woman. She also told them that she always dressed and acted like a lady.

A **SHARPSHOOTER** is a person who can shoot a gun and hit a target many times and very accurately.

ROSA PARKS (1913-2005):

Rosa Parks was a civil rights activist. She lived in Montgomery, Alabama at a time when people of color were not treated the same as white people. They were made to sit in different areas in restaurants and buses. They had to use different bathrooms, drinking fountains and even schools. Rosa and her husband did not think this was right. They belonged to a group called the National Association for the Advancement of Colored People (NAACP) that was trying to change things. On December 1, 1955, Rosa was riding the bus home from work. She was told to give up her seat for a white person. She refused. The bus driver had her arrested. This event brought all the black people of Montgomery together. They decided not to ride the bus until the laws were changed. This boycott lasted more than a year. The Supreme Court made a decision against the Montgomery rule and outlawed separate areas for different people on buses and trains. For the rest of her life, Rosa worked to teach about equal rights for all people.

An **ACTIVIST** is a person who fights for what they believe through protest, teaching, speeches and other means.

MARIE CURIE (1867-1934):

Marie Curie was a scientist who first learned how radiation works. She was born in Warsaw, Poland. Her parents were teachers and wanted her to go to school. The Russians were in charge and did not allow the Polish people to learn science. Marie wanted to go to school in France but her family did not have much money. Marie worked as a nanny and used her money to let her older sister go to school. When her sister finished her schooling, it was Marie's turn. She moved to Paris and went to the Sorbonne. She studied math and physics. She met her husband at school and they worked together doing research. Their work led to the discovery of two new elements. The elements were named radium and polonium. Also from their work, people began to understand radioactivity. Marie said that the radiation energy came from inside the atoms. Marie was the first woman awarded a Nobel Prize and the first woman to teach at the Sorbonne.

A **SCIENTIST** is a person who tries to understand and explain how things work. They may study animals, machines or rocks.

ELIZABETH BLACKWELL (1821-1910):

Elizabeth Blackwell was the first woman to go to school to become a doctor. She decided that she wanted to be a doctor after a sick friend said she was sad there were no women doctors to treat her. Elizabeth applied to more than 25 schools that said no to her. Finally, Geneva College in New York accepted her, if all her male classmates would agree. They may have thought it was a joke, but they said "Yes." Elizabeth finished first in her class in January 1849. She moved to France to practice. One day when she was giving eye medicine to a baby, an accident happened. Elizabeth lost her sight in one eye. Now she could not be a surgeon. Elizabeth went back to the United States but she still could not get a job as a doctor. Elizabeth opened a clinic for poor women and children that could not go to other doctors. She also started a medical school for women to learn to be doctors.

A **DOCTOR** is a person who knows how the body works. They help people who are hurt or sick. Doctors try to keep people healthy.

MOMMY:

Mommy was once a little girl with a big imagination and big dreams. Mom imagined growing up to be a princess, a firefighter, a dancer, an engineer, a teacher, a journalist, a professional roller skater, and more. She dreamed about having wonderful children and being a great mother. Now she is a wonderful mom and still has a big imagination. Mommy loves her children and gives them snuggly hugs. She is smart and funny and tells great stories.

A **MOTHER** is a person who uses love and wisdom to raise children to be caring, accomplished adults.

acknowledgements

I would like to thank all the women who strived to make changes in the world and allow me so many opportunities. I would also like to acknowledge the supremely talented Mike Litwin, who made this story come alive and invented a little girl who could have been me. My gratitude to Meredith Smith who assisted as a sounding-board, test Mom, marketing guru and all around cheerleader; to Paula who kept me on the straight and narrow; and to Sandra Duncan for her words. I am eternally grateful to the Alfonso family for doing all the dirty work and for my husband and family for always believing it could happen. **- JF**

list of works consulted

For more information on these and other exciting women check out the following:

BOOKS:

Adler, David and Robert Casilla (illustrator). A Picture Book of Rosa Parks (Picture Book Biography). New York: Holiday House, 1993.

Bennett, William J. (editor), and Michael Hague (illustrator). The Children's Book of Heroes. New York: Simon & Schuster Children's Publishing, 1997.

Cheney, Lynne and Robin Preiss Glasser (illustrator). A is for Abigail: An Almanac of Amazing American Women. New York: Simon & Schuster Children's Publishing, 2003.

Chin-Lee, Cynthia, Megan Helsy (illustrator) and Sean Addy (illustrator). Amelia to Zora: Twenty-Six Women Who Changed the World. Watertown: Charlesbridge Publishing, 2005.

Giovanni, Nikki and Bryan Collier (illustrator). Rosa. New York: Henry Holt and Company, 2005.

Gray, Gwendolyn. Girls Who Grew Up Great: A Book of Encouragement for Girls About Amazing Women Who Dared to Dream. Boulder: Blue Mountain Press, 2003.

Kishel, Ann-Marie. Elizabeth Blackwell: A Life of Diligence (Pull Ahead Books). Minneapolis: Lerner Publications Company, 2007.

Krensky, Stephen and Bernie Fuchs (illustrator). Shooting for the Moon: The Amazing Life and Times of Annie Oakley. New York: Farrar, Straus and Giroux, 2001.

Krull, Kathleen and Kathryn Hewitt (illustrator). Lives of Extraordinary Women: Rulers, Rebels (and What the Neighbors Thought). New York: Harcourt Children's Books, 2000.

Macy, Sue. Bull's-Eye: A Photobiography of Annie Oakley. Washington D.C.: National Geographic Children's Books, 2006.

Mader, Jan. Elizabeth Blackwell (First Biographies). Mankato: Pebble Books, 2007.

McDounough, Yona Zeldis and Mallah Zeldis (illustrator). Sisters in Strength: American Women who Made a Difference. New York: Henry Holt and Company, 2000.

Nichols, Catherine. Sally Ride (Scholastic News Nonfiction Readers). New York: Children's Press, 2005.

Parks, Rosa, Jim Haskins and Wil Clay. I Am Rosa Parks (Easy to Read). New York: Puffin, 1997.

Rau, Dana Meachen. Marie Curie (Compass Point Early Biographies). Mankato: Compass Point Books, 2000.

Raum, Elizabeth. Sally Ride (American Lives). Portsmouth: Heinemann, 2005.

Ride, Sally. To Space and Back. New York: Lothrop, Lee and Shepard Books, 1986.

Schaefer, Wyatt S. Marie Curie (First Biographies). Mankato: Capstone Press, 2004.

Steele, Philip. World History Biographies: Marie Curie: The Woman Who Changed the Course of Science. Washington D.C.: National Geographic Books, 2006.

Thimmesh, Catherine and Melissa Sweet (illustrator). Girls Think of Everything: Stories of Ingenious Inventions by Women. New York: Houghton Mifflin Company, 2000.

Willis, Charles M. Annie Oakley (DK Biography). New York: DK Children, 2007.

WEBSITES:

"Sally Kristen Ride: First American Woman in Space." Lucid Café Library: www.lucidcafe.com/library/96may/ride.html

"Biographical Data: Sally Ride." NASA: www.jsc.nasa.gov/Bios/htmlbios/ride-sk.html

"Annie Oakley: She Shot The Ashes Off The Kaiser's Cigaret." Cowgirl's Dream: www.cowgirls.com/dream/cowgals/oakley.htm

"Annie Oakley." Dorchester Library: www.dorchesterlibrary.org/library/aoakley.html

"Women in History: Annie Oakley." Lakewood Public Library: www.lkwdpl.org/wihohio/oakl-ann.htm

"Rosa Parks." Academy of Achievement: www.achievement.org/autodoc/page/par0bio-1

"Black History: Rosa Parks." GALE CENGAGE Learning: www.galegroup.com/free_resources/bhm/bio/parks_r.htm

"Spotlight on Mrs. Rosa Parks, Mother of the Civil Rights Movement." Girl Power! Guests: www.girlpower.gov/girlarea/gpguests/RosaParks.htm

"Rosa Louise Parks Biography." Rosa & Raymond Parks Institute for Self Development: www.rosaparks.org/bio.html

"Marie Curie." The AIP Center for History of Physics: www.aip.org/history/curie/

"Women's History: Marie Curie." GALE CENGAGE Learning: www.galegroup.com/free_resources/whm/bio/curie_m.htm

"Marie Curie." The Great Idea Finder: www.ideafinder.com/history/inventors/curie.htm

"Elizabeth Blackwell." About.com: Women's History: womenshistory.about.com/od/blackwellelizabeth/a/eliz_blackwell.htm

"Elizabeth Blackwell (1821-1910)." Biography.com: www.biography.com/search/article.do?id=9214198

"Women's History: Elizabeth Blackwell." GALE CENGAGE Learning: www.galegroup.com/free_resources/whm/bio/blackwell_e.htm

"Elizabeth Blackwell, MD." Wellness Directory of Minnesota: www.mnwelldir.org/docs/history/biographies/blackwell.htm

Info Please: All the Knowledge you need: www.infoplease.com/people.html